Felicity

Shines

Written by Kylie Manning
Illustrated by Randy Kopka

ISBN-13: 978-0692153840
ISBN-10: 0692153845

Felicitations

For Allison and Ashley, of course. You are my sunshines.

Thanks to God for teaching me the lesson of this story and inspiring me to share it with others. I give Him all the glory.

Thanks to my parents who first taught me how to be creative and believe in myself.

Dad, you'll always be my favorite artist. Thanks for illustrating. You brought my story to life!

Mom, your words of wisdom have always been the inspiration for my best work.

Thanks to Allan for believing I'm shining even when I can't see it. I love you.

Thanks to Mrs. Sharon Mack, my first grade reading teacher, who told my mother I would be an author someday.

One late summer afternoon, Felicity the firefly left home and headed out to greet her friends in the forest. Felicity had always been taught to be humble, to never think or act as though she were better than anyone else. She practiced this every day and, over time, she made a habit of seeing the good in all she crossed paths with. Because of this, she had many friends.

First, she came upon Timothy the tadpole swimming in a mud puddle.

"Hi, Timothy! How are you? Wow! How you are growing! Look at your legs! They weren't there the last time I saw you!" Felicity cheered.

"I'm well, thanks," Timothy replied. "It won't be long until I can leap right out of this puddle!"

"That's terrific, Timothy! I'm so proud of you!" Felicity encouraged. She couldn't see it, but each time she showed kindness, her belly lit up!

The friends visited for some time, but then Felicity said, "Goodbye, Timothy! I must see more of my friends before it gets dark! My mama will be expecting me to be home!"

"Bluh-blye!" Timothy bubbled through the muck.

As she flew away, Felicity actually felt quite sad. She was happy to see her friend, and each time she saw him she was more and more amazed with his growth and ability. She thought to herself, "I'll never be able to leap like him."

Soon, Felicity fled to a nearby stream. The brook was babbling so loud she could hardly hear Bailey the beaver calling her name.

"Felicity! Felicity! Come and look at what I just made!" Bailey shouted.

Felicity flew over and saw the most magnificent structure of branches, sticks, and mud she had ever seen.

"This is incredible, Bailey! You did a great job!" Felicity exclaimed as she looked at the dam.

She still couldn't see it, but her belly was shining even more brightly as she thought those happy thoughts and said those caring words.

The friends conversed, but then it was time to fly.

"I'll see you later, Bailey! It's starting to get dark!" Felicity remarked.

As she flew away, Felicity thought to herself. "I can't build anything like that! I wish I could be like Bailey. I wish I could be like Timothy! They have so much to offer the world and I have nothing."

As Felicity headed home through the woods, she heard a beautiful song from a familiar voice.

"Is that you, Christopher?" she asked.

As she looked ahead, she could see his vibrant red feathers spiking up from his head. Christopher the cardinal was resting on a branch, effortlessly singing the most splendid tune Felicity had ever heard.

"It is I, my dear," Christopher chirped.

Felicity landed beside him.

"That was astounding! Sing some more!" Felicity eagerly requested.

Christopher smiled and sang again.

Felicity felt her spirits lift as she enjoyed the melody. Her underside, still where she could not see, illuminated more brightly than before.

"Thank you for your wonderful performance, Christopher! You have a true gift!" Felicity kindly replied as she departed. "I'll be back for another visit soon!"

As she hurried along, she couldn't help but feel a deep ache inside. She sincerely loved and admired her friends. They had such unique qualities that made them so extraordinary. She wanted so desperately to feel special too. "It seems like everyone has a talent except for me," she thought.

It wasn't long until the sky was dark. Felicity could see the moon and stars sparkling in the night sky. There, she found her mother resting on a blade of grass in a field. Felicity landed beside her.

"Well, hello, my darling child. How was your adventure?" her mother questioned.

"It was great!" Felicity replied with a smile, but it quickly turned into a frown.

"I can tell something is wrong," Felicity's mother noticed. "What is troubling you?" she asked.

"Mama, I had a fantastic time with my friends today. Timothy the tadpole will soon leave the puddle! He has all four legs now! Bailey the beaver made an awesome dam all by herself! Christopher the cardinal sang me the most beautiful song I've ever heard!" All the while, Felicity's belly was beaming with a stunning yellow-green radiance.

Felicity continued, "I love my friends for all the lovely gifts they have to offer, but it makes me feel badly about *me*."

Suddenly, Felicity's belly stopped shining.

Her mother took Felicity into her large, black wings and said, "Oh, sweetheart, I wish you could see how you truly shine as brilliantly as the stars tonight because you have so much love and admiration for others. When you love and respect others and look for the good in them, your belly glows brighter than you can see. Everyone else can see it and it uplifts all of us. I'm sorry, love. When I taught you that you are not better than anyone else, I should have also taught you that no one is better than you either."

After hearing that, Felicity felt truly peaceful inside. As she sat on a blade of grass by the meadow pond, she saw her own light shining brightly in her reflection in the water for the very first time.

"Wow, it does look like the stars like Mama said! I do have a gift! A light to shine for others!" she thought joyfully. She finally knew, without a doubt, that she had a special place, too. And, ever since, Felicity started a new habit. Every time she thought, said, or did something lovely to help another, she looked for a smile on another's face, but also for her own light shining… and that made her feel shiny on the inside, too. Marvelously, now, it was beaming greater than ever because she didn't leave any room for bad thoughts, words, or deeds, even toward herself. She loved others and was loved in return by many. Even if someone didn't love her, she would still let her light shine. Finally, she knew for sure, that seeing the good in others took nothing away from her own good. In fact, seeing the good in others brings out the good in her, too!

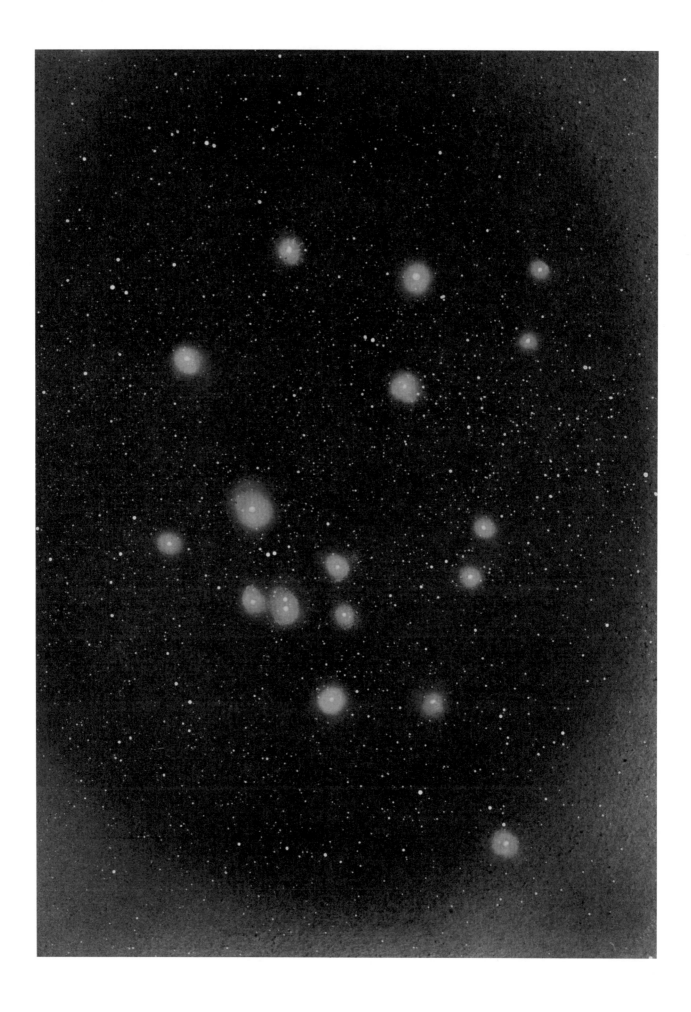

About the Author

Kylie Manning is the illustrator's daughter. She is a devoted wife of Allan and mother of two daughters. She is also a physical therapist assistant. She enjoys home making, art, music, long walks, gardening, reading, and spending time with her children and other friends and family in the great outdoors. She hopes to inspire all of her readers to choose good thoughts, do good deeds, and to never forget what a gift they are to the world every day.

About the Illustrator

Randy Kopka is the author's father. He is a machinist by trade with a degree in graphic art and design. He has been drawing since a very young age.

"I pray that the images do the story justice.
For my Wife, Children, and Grandchildren. I love you."

God Bless.

42848868R00015

Made in the USA
Middletown, DE
17 April 2019